This book belongs to

....

For Tabitha Constance Rose, my own smiling schoolgirl,

with love from Mama – LC

Dorling **DK** Kindersley

LONDON, NEW YORK, SYDNEY, DELHI, PARIS,
MUNICH and JOHANNESBURG

First published in Great Britain in 2000 by
Dorling Kindersley Limited,
9 Henrietta Street, London WC2E 8PS

2 4 6 8 10 9 7 5 3 1

Text copyright © 2000 Lucy Coats
Illustrations copyright © 2000 Emily Bolam
The author's and illustrator's moral rights have been asserted.

A CIP catalogue record for this book is available from the British Library.

ISBN 0-7513-7258-7

Colour reproduction by Dot Gradations, UK
Printed in China by South China Press

see our complete
catalogue at
www.dk.com

One Smiling Sister

Lucy Coats

Illustrated by Emily Bolam

A Dorling Kindersley Book

ONE smiling sister – bowl and spoon and cup.

Pour the milk and stir it round.

YUMMY! Eat it up!

TWO twins in a rush – hats and gloves can wait!

Backpacks on and coats done up.

HURRY! We'll be late!

THREE little chatty girls on their way to play.

Look! Some ducks! A cow! A horse!

MOO! MOO! Quack! Quack! NEIGH!

FOUR teachers counting heads – Jo and John and Jan.

Sam and Sarah, Kate and Carrie –

Look! At last! Here's Dan.

FIVE pots of pretty paint, coloured paper too.

Everybody's drawn a tiger

For our classroom zoo.

SIX doughnuts left to eat. Is there one for John?

Grabbing hands and sticky faces –

Soon they'll all be gone.

SEVEN skipping kangaroos coming out to play.

Kate hops highest, Jan's all jumpy.

Watch them bounce! **Hooray!**

EIGHT children sitting still. Now we can begin.

Will the wolf chase all the pigs?

Or will the piggies win?

NINE fingers pointing up, reaching very high.

Twinkle, twinkle, little star!

Let's all touch the sky.

TEN happy mums and dads take a tiny peek.

Children running, lots of waving.

See you all next week!

Other Toddler Books to collect:

MY DO IT!
by Ros Asquith, illustrated by Sam Williams

BALL!
by Ros Asquith, illustrated by Sam Williams

PANDA BIG AND PANDA SMALL
by Jane Cabrera

RORY AND THE LION
by Jane Cabrera

HERE COMES THE RAIN
by Mary Murphy

CATERPILLAR'S WISH
by Mary Murphy

BABY LOVES
*by Michael Lawrence,
illustrated by Adrian Reynolds*

BABY LOVES HUGS AND KISSES
*by Michael Lawrence,
illustrated by Adrian Reynolds*

TING-A-LING!
by Siobhan Dodds

THE PIG WHO WISHED
by Joyce Dunbar, illustrated by Selina Young

GRUMBLE-RUMBLE!
by Siobhan Dodds

NED'S RAINBOW
by Melanie Walsh

HIDE AND SLEEP
by Melanie Walsh

I'M TOO BUSY
by Helen Stephens

WHAT ABOUT ME?
by Helen Stephens

SILLY GOOSE AND DAFT DUCK
PLAY HIDE-AND-SEEK
*by Sally Grindley,
illustrated by Adrian Reynolds*

GRANDMA RABBITTY'S VISIT
by Barry Smith